Also available from Griffinwing Publishing:

in ebook (complete trilogy):
Running Out Of Space (Sunblinded #1)
Dying For Space (Sunblinded #2)
Breathing Space (Sunblinded #3)
Sunblinded – The Complete Trilogy box set

in paperback:
Running Out Of Space (Sunblinded #1)
Dying for Space (Sunblinded #2)
Breathing Space (Sunblinded #3)

The Arcadian Chronicles in ebook
Mantivore Dreams (The Arcadian Chronicles #1)
Mantivore Prey (The Arcadian Chronicles #2)
Mantivore Warrior (The Arcadian Chronicles #3)

Available from Grimbold Publishing
Netted – a standalone novel

PICKY EATERS

PICKY EATERS
A SHORT STORY

S. J. Higbee

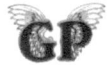

Published by Griffinwing Publishing

First published as a 1,000 short story at Every Day Fiction, 2009

ISBN: 978-1-911139-24-9

Cover art donated by
Mhairi Simpson

Griffinwing Publishing

www.sjhigbee.com

DEDICATION

To all those who have been alongside me during my
struggles with Long Covid –
you know who you are – thank you so much.

All proceeds raised by this story will be donated to
Mental Health Charities.

I - Picky Eaters

He came to with a sudden awareness that he must have dozed off, which was happening more often these days. Still, no harm done… He stretched and yawned, choosing to ignore the patter of dirt falling from his crusted scales. Only as he started to curl up, ready to turn the nap into a proper mid-morning snooze, did he recall he was supposed to be babysitting his pesky grandchildren. Where'd they got to?

Once he located the youngsters huddled in the corner, he decided Billy Bob and Sammy Jo were up to something, so he tip-taloned across the cavern, before whispering, "What are you doing?" in Billy Bob's ear.

The small dragon shot straight into the air with a shrill squeal, while his sister crouched lower over whatever-it-was in the gloom, gobbling it up in a couple of hurried gulps.

An irritated wisp of smoke leaked from his nostrils. "And *why* are you eating between meals?"

"'Um unngree…" she mumbled, still chewing.

The delicious whiff of a meaty something didn't improve his temper. "If you'd eaten all your breakfast, you wouldn't be wanting something, now!"

"Sorry, Granddad," Billy Bob whimpered, his wings drooping submissively.

But young Sammy Jo was made of sterner stuff. Her wings remained neatly folded across her back as she announced, "Didn't like breakfast."

Impudent little piece! Why, when he was a dragonet, if he'd spoken to a lord so insolently, he'd have been walking around with singed scales for a month. Smoke now was trickling steadily from his nostrils, as he growled, "And what does *like* have to do with anything? Answer that one, miss! There's sub-Saharan dragons who'd give their wings for a tasty morsel like the one I picked out for you."

"They can have it, then," Sammy Jo said sulkily. "It tasted funny."

The rank ingratitude! His temper flared, and a gout of flame belched out of his mouth with his roar, "Ahh!"

She dodged his fiery blast with ease. "You can't singe us, Granddad. It's not allowed." Sammy Jo stretched her neck in an unmistakeably female way. "If we've been bad, we have to sit on the naughty crag and think about what we've done wrong and how to make a-mends."

He regarded her with smouldering annoyance. "You sound just like your grandmother."

"I w-want Mummee!" wailed Billy Bob, an acrid smell of damp charcoal settling around the dragonet.

Sammy Jo wrapped a foreleg around the howling infant. "Shh, Bills. Mummy'll be here, soon." Flashing a baleful glare at him, she added, "She won't like it that you made Billy Bob cry. *And* she said we didn't have to eat any of your tinned food if we didn't want to. So there."

"Want Mummee. Want nice din-dins…"

He raised his voice over Billy Bob's piercing squeals, "Your precious mother didn't think to bring anything with her, I notice."

Sammy Jo's answer was on the insufferable side of smug, "Mummy didn't have to. Billy Bob and me hunt for ourselves."

"S'right," snivelled Billy Bob, starting to cheer up.

He snorted, all set to be contemptuously amused. "Oh yes? And when did you go off hunting, then?"

"When you fell asleep. After you ate up all the breakfast."

"I did *not* fall asleep – as you put it, miss." He was uncomfortably aware that if Sammy Jo presented his teeny power-nap in such terms to his daughter, she would probably have far too much to say, in that bossy trumpeting bugle of hers, "I merely closed my eyes to meditate. It's what dragon lords do, once they reach a certain age."

"Tinned food is yucky." He almost preferred Billy Bob's howling to his perky cheekiness. Almost.

Meanwhile Sammy Jo was in full flow, "Mummy says it isn't natural to shut the food up in a can. It should be fresh and free range. That's what Mummy tells us. Then we'll grow up big and healthy."

"Well, that just goes to show how much your mother knows, then," he snapped, "because my tinned food is so fresh and free range, it climbs right to the top of my mountain."

Sammy Jo put her head to one side. "Why?"

He knew exactly why those tin-suited would-be murderers regularly struggled up to his lair and attacked him, forcing him to eventually flame them. But he wasn't prepared to share the whole grim story with little missy, here. "Because they want to be eaten." The lie sounded unconvincing, even to him.

"Ours don't," Billy Bob boasted. "Our food runned away. And we knock them – boff! Over they goed – wriggly, wiggly on the ground. And they squealed... Like this." The dragonet squirmed around on the floor, making bleating yells.

Sammy Jo giggled as she watched her small brother making those wailing noises, which sounded like...

A dreadful thought occurred to him. "This food of yours – where did you get it?"

"The food we caught lives in those boxes sprouting in the valley. We don't have food growing like that at Wyvern Crag. Up there, it's mostly birds and mountain goats. But here, your food moves slowly and stays near the boxes. Mostly it was too big for us, so we chose the two littlest ones." His granddaughter half closed her eyes in remembered bliss. "Mm. So juicy."

He hadn't felt so afraid since the day his mate deserted him, two centuries earlier. Rushing to the entrance of his lair, he looked down the mountainside. The food was upset, alright. They'd bunched together in a large crowd and were funnelling up the road towards the mountain. His mountain.

Over the years, a dragon lord learns many useful things. He'd learnt to instantly count to thirty-nine during his seven-hundred-and-twenty-one-year-old life. And why thirty-nine? Because in his prime, that was the maximum number of these creatures he could kill in one go. Looking down the mountain, he realised that there were a *lot* more than thirty-nine food items marching towards his aery, variously armed with nasty-looking implements. If he'd been alone, he would have faced the whole flock of them. Gone out fighting as befitted an old warrior lord. But now, with children in his care that wasn't an option.

Snarling a foul curse that had Sammy Jo widening her eyes and murmuring how Mummy didn't like naughty words, he grabbed Billy Bob in a gnarled claw and turned to Sammy Jo. "Fly! We're headed toward Wyvern Peak. To find you a naughty crag." Swinging out over the sheer drop, he extended his tattered wings.

"Where you pesky lizards can sit till you figure how to recover my lair!"

II – Birds, Bees and Baby Boulders

In his daughter's cramped guest chamber, he was trying to doze. But the squabble next door wasn't helping. How the blazes was a dragon lord supposed to snooze with *that* going on?

"No, we can't— Rondell... **I said NO.**"

There was a muffled yelp from Rondell – or as he thought of him, 'that waste of skin and scales'. He shifted, fervently grateful that all the complicated stuff between a dragon lord and queen was now behind him.

"Didn't have to use your claws, babe. I would've backed off." Rondell's reproachful whine dropped to a sub-sonic growl, "Let's take the children with us. We could play a game of hide and seek and just slip off for..."

Emmy Lou snorted. "Can you *imagine* taking Sammy Jo on a mating flight, with that knack of hers of always turning up at the wrong time?" She mimicked her daughter's piercing tones, "Mummy, what's Daddy doing, now?"

As the air suddenly cleared of mating pheromones, he

gratefully sucked in a clean lungful. It had been getting quite intense in the lair. And not in a good way. He was sure that back in his day, when he'd been interested in all that... business, his pheromones had smelt more alluring and less like mouldy old talon clippings.

"Made your point," Rondell sounded sulky, in the neighbouring chamber. "Not that packing them off to your dad's got us anywhere, did it? Useless old carcass even managed to mess that up. And now we're landed with him cluttering up the place."

He shook with rage. Small wonder standards were sliding down the mountainside into a stake-lined pit, when scrawny little—

"Never mind about Father. There should be an egg in the hatchery, by now. And just what are you doing about it?" Emmy-Lou sounded frighteningly like her mother.

The trouble with Wyvern Peak were all the memories that kept popping to the surface. Small wonder he wasn't getting enough rest, he grumped to himself, while stomping into the main chamber.

"Eh?" He stopped, as if surprised to see them. "Thought you two would be long gone by now."

"There's not enough time. The children are due back from the crèche, Father," Emmy Lou said slowly. As if he was deaf, or stupid. Or both.

He waved a foreleg. "I'll look after them. Get going. You'll want to be back before sunset."

Emmy Lou shrugged off Rondell's eager grasp. "You're sure, Dad?"

"Of course." He couldn't resist a slitted glance at Rondell. "Thought I'd start teaching them chess." Which he knew Rondell couldn't play.

The waste of skin and scales didn't know how to behave when an alpha lord was under his roof, either. He noticed it was Emmy Lou thanking him to the skies and back, as the pair rushed for the exit in unseemly haste, while Rondell shifted his wings across his back and mumbled something under his breath like a naughty dragonet. But then he was well aware that he always disconcerted his son-in-law.

His grin faded as he heard the clamorous arrival of those pesky nuisances from the crèche, and Sammy Jo's shrill voice echoing around the aery, "Mummy, what's a rep-reputation? Teacher says that Granddad has one."

*

They'd scratched a chessboard in the dirt, before Sammy Jo started, "Mummy says that only grown-ups have mating flights."

"Wanna mating flight," whined Billy Bob.

"We need stones this shape, scatterling." He waved a pebble at him. "For our chess pieces."

Distracted, Billy Bob happily scuffled through rock fragments.

Sammy Jo's bright gaze skewered him, as she said, "Mummy says after the mating flight, there'll be an egg." She tilted her head. "How does that happen?"

Yearning for the good old-fashioned phrases of his youth, like 'Wait and see', his mind blanked. "Um... you know the birds and bees?"

Her brow-ridge wrinkled. "Do they go on mating flights, too?"

His desperate glance rested on Billy Bob's mound of stones. "Well, there's baby boulders..."

"And you bash a big boulder to make baby boulders."

Sammy Jo's eyes widened. "Is *that* how it happens?"

"Something like that. Now here's our Dragon Queen and Overlord, and they go just here…" He congratulated himself on a nifty subject change, as Sammy Jo picked up basic chess moves impressively fast. Clever little thing. For a nuisance.

Just over three hours later, when the glowing couple returned from their tryst, he basked in their gratitude. After Emmy Lou had laid her egg and retired to rest, he even felt magnanimous enough to escort the dragonets into the hatchery to see it.

"There's only one, though." Sammy Jo peered at the glowing egg in the nest.

"Want more," whined Billy Bob, waving a stone around.

"Don't be so ungrateful, you wretched little lizards," he snapped, deciding he'd had far too much family time. "I'm off for a rest."

Rondell muttered grudging thanks, looking like he'd rather slice off his tongue.

While Sammy Jo suddenly launched into the air, and fluttering around his head, wafted affectionate breaths of steam in his face, closely followed by Billy Bob. "Night, night Granddad. Me and Billy Bob, we like it that you're staying with us, don't we, Bills?" The dragonets' huge eyes, so close to his, along with their achingly sweet scent brought back a raft of memories of when Emmy Lou had been that age. Memories that pierced him with the sharpness of a lance.

"Mm," said Billy Bob, less convinced.

Clearing his throat, which seemed to have become unaccountably tight, he mumbled that they'd better sleep well, before he headed for the guest chamber feeling he'd earned a good long snooze.

*

The scream jerked him into the hatchery before he was properly awake.

A *terrible* scream. The kind a female makes when mortally injured or – or –

Not Sammy Jo! The thought blazed through his sleep-silted head like a fireball.

It wasn't Sammy Jo. Or Billy Bob.

They were cowering by the smashed egg. Looking up at their distraught parents with wide, unblinking eyes. Billy Bob gripped a yoke-smeared stone in his trembling fore-claw while Rondell drooled burning saliva, trying to control his rage.

Staring at the scene, he realised he'd left the dragonets with the notion that if they broke the egg into pieces, there'd be more brothers.

My fault. Another revelation streaking through his head. Bringing with it a sequence of physical sensations he'd Vowed never to experience again.

His temperature plummeted.

By the time he had reduced Rondell's molten dribble to a sputtering icicle, he was cold enough to scramble over frost-rimed minutes.

"Whee! This is fun…"

He couldn't believe his ears. It took several long, frozen seconds of blinking to actually trust his eyes. *I must be seeing things…*

But she was all too solid as Sammy Jo slithered down yet another minute and fetched up against his leg, giggling and panting. "Why are the others standing still, like that? Ooo – you're all frosty, Granddad! Just like an Ice Giant like in the stories Teacher tells."

"Come on!" he snapped. "You'll have to come with me – I can't leave you here." *Or you'll be stuck amongst the solidified minutes and swallowed up as I travel forward, again.*

Easier said than done, though. He held his breath as she flung herself over each ice-bound moment, sliding down the curved side of every frozen mound on her belly... her back... And in one horrifying example, on the underside of a wing that – somehow – became folded inside out. Though she scrambled back up with no apparent harm, all set to do it again, her eyes glittering with excitement.

So it took a lot longer than he'd planned to reach the frigid moment when Billy Bob raised his stone over the intact egg.

"What're you doing, Granddad? Oh! Will that stop Billy Bob hurting the egg? Ooo – lemme take the stone away. Please, please, please," she clamoured, still skittering across the tops of solid seconds as if she'd been born to it.

"Go on, then!" he growled, wishing he had half her energy to waste.

As she snatched the stone out of Billy Bob's claw, he delicately picked him up and carried the dragonet back to his sleeping mound in the nursery. Then scooped up his granddaughter, who'd been skittering around the frozen lair. He wrapped his tail around her, so that his forelegs were free, keeping her as far away as he could from the melting moments and any risk of being swept away by the rushing time-stream.

There wasn't time to explain what needed to happen next. The bit he dreaded. The bit that *hurt*. His agonised roars shook the walls as he raced forward to the present. Dimly he heard Sammy Jo squealing as she wriggled within his coils. But he was too busy concentrating on arriving back at exactly the right spot to explain what was happening. Besides, he doubted that he was able to do anything other than whimper if he opened his mouth.

Gritting his teeth against the pain as his temperature shot back to somewhere approaching normal, he shook condensation from his steaming scales. Sammy Jo slipped out from his grasp as the desperate family tableau unfroze.

"It's only a nightmare..." he felt as sick as a half-eaten hog by the time his explanation had seeped through Emmy-Lou's shocked grief; he'd snarled a threat at Rondell, as that waste of skin and scales was still teetering on the brink of flaming the spot where his young son had been standing. And – finally – he staggered off to the nursery to pick up a keening Billy Bob and jig him into silence, whereupon the small dragonet promptly fell asleep while cradled in his forelegs. He'd then rounded up his granddaughter, hoping her parents hadn't noticed that she was gently steaming as she'd danced around their legs, warbling with excitement.

However Emmy Lou was in no fit state to notice anything as, still shaking, she allowed Rondell to guide her back to their sleeping chamber. "C'mon babe... Must've been all the emotion – what with our flight... then laying the egg..." her mate's voice faded into a muffled growl as the couple stumbled away.

He tottered from the hatchery, ready to tip the dragonet back into her sleeping mound. But Sammy Jo scrabbled out of his grasp, swarmed up his neck and perched on the folds of his crest. "You *are* cold. So it *wasn't* just a dream like you told Mummy and Daddy! We did turn everything all frosty and pulled everything backwards to unbreak the egg!" The small female wasn't even shivering, though she felt far too cold.

His stomach slithered to somewhere around his knees, as he tried to work out how she could possibly have inherited his ability to freeze time. Such a rare talent, he was the only surviving dragon who possessed it.

How could she...? He knew there were other major questions he needed to consider, but right now his brain had lurched to a standstill. All he could do was slowly shake his head.

"I'm not wrong! It can't have been a dream. See? I still got the stone!" She waved it about.

"Shh! Don't you wake up your brother, you pesky little nuisance!" But even as he growled at her, his crest flicked approval at her exuberance.

Destined to be a golden green like her mother, Sammy Jo was glowing with excitement. "Ooo... that *was* fun!" Her black tongue flicked out, pattering his scales with affection. "I *like* you Granddad – it's *nice* you're staying here. That was *lovely*..."

Billy Bob squirmed and opened bleary eyes. "Sammy? Wanna play..." he slurred, before flopping back on his sleep mound, abruptly asleep again. So he gently heaped up a pile of coins over his tiny grandson, freeing a firestorm of memories of other times he'd tucked up sleepy dragonets.

"Granddad?" Sammy Jo's piercing whisper was almost as loud as her normal voice.

He scowled down at her. "Don't you wake up your brother, miss! You hear me?"

She beamed up at him, once more flicking her tongue out, fondly. "Course I can hear you, Granddad. You're here. Cuddling me..." She relaxed in his arms for a space of several heartbeats.

His head nodded in exhaustion. That was the trouble with time-travel. It took it out of you...

"Granddad! Should you fall asleep over Billy Bob? Do you crash onto your side like Daddy does? Or do you keep swaying like that?"

He jerked awake, horrified that he'd come within a fire worm's hair of flattening his grandson and injuring this precious child in his arms. "Come on, miss..." He ached all over as he tottered to the guest chamber, still cradling Sammy Jo. Muscles he'd forgotten he had were screaming curses at his abuse. At his age he shouldn't be gallivanting around, time-travelling. He should be curled up in his lair over Devastation Valley, keeping watch on the old rift, while waiting for the food to finally overwhelm him in battle.

However there wasn't time for such introspection. He might have been exhausted as he slumped onto his sleeping mound, but young Sammy Jo certainly wasn't.

"Ooo... that was *such* fun! Can we do it again, Granddad? And next time, can we take Billy Bob? Please, please, please? He'd *love* it. And I'd take good care of him. Make sure he doesn't get in the way. Me and Billy Bob – we make a good team. Mummy says so…" The young dragon was vibrating with excitement – and something else…

Something he recognised with a mixture of dread and resignation, recalling his first time-travelling journey as if it were yesterday. And the fierce sense that *this* was what he was born to do… He also remembered, with a wince, how impatient he'd been with poor old Grimwurt, the elderly lord who'd escorted him on his earliest time-travels, before expiring with the effort halfway through their twenty-sixth sortie, together. Another outing forever branded onto his memory, for all the wrong reasons.

What if I'd died halfway through this last caper? He looked down at the youngster flitting around his tattered wings, and shivered. *She wouldn't have stood a chance of getting back!* Then pulled himself together. After all, he was a relative youngster compared to Grimwurt, who'd been nudging nine hundred years old when he'd stumbled over a frozen month in mid-stride before plummeting into the crevice between two icy year-cliffs.

He took a breath. "We can't take Billy Bob. For starters, he's too little. I know it seemed like fun, but it can be very dangerous. And…" His exhausted brain struggled to find the right words, "Very few dragons can freeze time. Ever. In all my life I've only ever known a few dragons who could do it. And all but one other is dead."

Sammy Jo tilted her head on one side, her huge eyes swirling with emotion. "So it wasn't Daddy… or Grandma… Was he Wendell Bo's Daddy?"

His crest flicked in pleased surprise – he'd known she was bright! "No… Wendell Bo's daddy wasn't the

Overlord in those days." *Back then, the dragon lords would've had a scrawny little wretch like Wendell Bo and his puny bloodline for a mid-morning snack if he'd had the arrogance to duel for leadership!*

"So why can't I tell everyone? It's *such* fun…" She was zipping around the confined chamber, all but scampering up the walls in her excitement.

He hesitated, storing up her joy for a handful of precious moments, before he had to spoil it all. "Well, let's imagine you're a bit more grown up and everyone gets to know about your time-travelling abilities. Say that a group of lords don't like the way Wendell Bo is leading the Wyvern Peak aery…"

You'd have to be a brain-lamed cave slug to think he's doing a competent job, after all. "They might come to you and say, 'Sammy Jo, we'll give you a fresh-dug emerald if you freeze time, go back to when Wendell Bo was given the job and make sure that…" He tried to think of any suitable dragon up to the task of being Overlord, from the scruffy shower of lords littering the place. And couldn't. "…that someone else becomes Leader of Wyvern Peak, instead."

Sammy Jo stopped her capering. Her huge eyes glowed, as she stared across the guest chamber, thinking so hard he could almost taste her effort.

Finally she said, "That's not right. Daddy doesn't like Overlord Wendell Bo. But he says that he's the best of a slack-winged batch. And everyone *agreed* on Overlord Wendell Bo's bloodline." She stretched her neck and resettled her wings. "So I'd tell them, 'No. I won't do it.'"

He nodded. "Good. That's a wise thing to say.

But…" His heart hurt as he watched the innocence blazing from the small dragonet. Innocence he was about to ruin. "What if those lords and their friends are very angry? They know you can do it. So they grab Billy Bob or Mummy. Fly away with them somewhere. And tell you that if you don't do what they want – they'll kill them. What will you do, then?"

"They wouldn't… would they?" Her voice was small and pleading, her eyes shocked.

"To live in Pinnacle Point? To get first pick of every hunt? To decide whose bloodline can continue? That's a lot of power, Kindling." The pet name fell out of his mouth and his tongue stroked her brow-ridge, trying to offer some comfort for his cruel words. "And there's some around here who'd kill their sleeping mothers for a chance at such power." He shut his eyes, finding the sight of Sammy Jo's distress too much to bear as her wings drooped and she blinked in shock.

He recalled one ancient lord – was it Grimwurt? – telling him the worst bit about getting *really* old was that hurts became sharper with repetition. Until they swamped all the joys, which – somehow – only stayed the same. During the last two hundred years, he'd pondered upon that particular comment a great deal.

"Why don't you settle down and sleep, now? You can stay here. No point in returning to the nursery and disturbing Billy Bob." He rested his head on a handy boulder before it fell off his neck with weariness, and coiled his tail, trying not to wince as countless muscles and scuffs protested. "Look. I've made a nest so you can warm up some more…" his voice drifted off as he fell into heavy sleep.

PICKY EATERS

III – Shiny Scales and Unwelcome Visitors

"Samantha Joanna of Wyvern Peak! *What* have you done to Granddad?"

He jerked awake at his daughter's trumpeting bugle. It took him a long sleep-sodden moment to work out why he wasn't in his habitual lair. And why Emmy Lou would be stomping into his sleeping chamber.

"Doesn't he look *lovely*?" Sammy Jo's voice brought it all rushing back.

Though his eyelids still refused to open, as she continued, "I wasn't tired last night after... the egg thing. So Granddad brought me into his sleeping chamber so I wouldn't disturb Billy Bob."

"Well, he'll be regretting *that* decision when he sees what you've gone and done!" snapped his daughter.

Reminding him just how moody females could be when incubating an egg.

"Why?" Even with closed eyes he could visualise Sammy Jo's characteristic head tilt as she asked yet another impertinent, penetrating question.

"Because it looks ridiculous!" shrilled Emmy Lou.

He winced, hoping that Sammy Jo would agree with her aggravated mother and leave him in peace to slide back into sleep...

But this was Sammy Jo, who didn't ever agree with anyone just for an easy life. "No it doesn't – it looks wonderful! Better than anyone else in Wyvern Peak. I always thought he was just a scruffy old grey. But look, Mummy – just look! In that patch where I cleaned him up – he's black. A real black!"

What! Snapping both sets of eyelids open, he swung round to face his glowing granddaughter.

Who scampered up to him, affectionately flicking out her small tongue and swathing his head in an outpouring of loving steam. "Hallo, Granddad! Look what I did while you were sleeping. Don't you look just *lovely*?" Her huge eyes were swirling with excitement.

He slowly turned his head, the previous day's exertions leaving his whole body stiff and sore. She *had* been busy. Because right in the middle of his long, grey, dirt-scurfed flank was a patch twice her length, maybe, where his ebony scales gleamed. He stared in appalled fascination. How long had it been since he'd seen his scales that midnight black? Their obsidian hue glittered with flecks of bronze, silver and gold he'd ingested over his long lifetime. And even as he stared – as his lordly pride exulted in their sheer beauty – his heart thumped with shocked fear. Something of his feelings must have shown, though he was still too shaken to emit smoke.

"Granddad, aren't you pleased?" Sammy Jo's voice suddenly sounded thin and uncertain.

"Sammy Jo – come to me. At once!" Emmy Lou snapped, her wings half raised in clear threat and smoke wisping from her nostrils.

"Go and fly off that thunderstorm of a mood you're carrying around with you, Emmeline Louisa!" he snarled, summoning up every ounce of alpha lord he possessed. "If you think I'd flame the child for an honest mistake, then it's past time you took off for a long flight till you're fit to think with a clear head!"

She resettled her wings, her crest bristling with sarcasm. "Oh, *I'm* the one that needs a clear head, am I? You *can't* be seen like that! I won't have the rest of the aery sniggering up a firestorm at your appearance. Not on top of all the other—" Emmy Lou broke off and swung round to her daughter. "And never mind about your precious grandfather not flaming you. I'm *this* close to giving you a good old-fashioned singeing! Have you any idea how long it's going to take to get the rest of him clean?" His daughter's bugle reached an ear-piercing screech.

Which woke up the waste of skin and scales. "Babe! What's wrong? Is it the egg?" Rondell rushed into the sleeping chamber so quickly, he narrowly avoided crashing into his mate. Typical. He'd seen drunken elephants display more grace than that undersized loser.

Who snorted gouts of fire-spattered laughter when he saw the problem. "Serves him right for letting his scales get in that state in the first place! C'mon, babe. Get some rest. You shouldn't be worrying about this stuff. Not with an egg in the hatchery."

"Of course I shouldn't! Who knows how this stress will affect our unborn son!"

He rolled his eyes. Emmy Lou had her mother's tendency to get over-dramatic. Tedious enough in a mate, but plain annoying in a daughter.

"It didn't take all that long last night. Not really," piped up Sammy Jo. "Why don't you let me and Granddad stay here for the day, cleaning him up? I can go to the crèche tomorrow, instead."

"If I were you, I'd keep quiet for once in your short life," snapped Rondell. "It's gonna take days and days of hard scrubbing to get the rest of his huge bulk shining like that— Hey, is that silver? And gold – wow!" Rondell shouldered Emmy Lou out of the way and actually *peered* at the patch of clean scales.

As if he were some mutant food type.

"How old did you say he was?" the idiot runt muttered in a hoarse whisper to Emmy Lou.

Who glared back at him. "Go soak yourself, Rondell!" She turned back to Sammy Jo. "Unlike your father, I happen to think you should have to deal with the consequences of your actions. It was your bright idea to polish up Granddad's scales. So yes – you can spend the day finishing what you've started. And then we'll discuss exactly how many more days, evenings or fly-time you'll be spending over the next weeks on this task."

"Yes, Mummy," replied Sammy Jo, for once, suitably chastened by Emmy Lou's evident rage.

"Don't know why you've jumped to the conclusion that I want to be cleaned up!" he snapped, thoroughly fed up with being treated like a dirty latrine. "It'd be far easier to simply roll in the dust until that patch matches the rest of my body."

Emmy Lou snorted. "Oh good luck with that one, Father! I may not know much about much, but I've spent far too many hours polishing scales. And I'm here to tell you there's no way you'll manage to blend that patch with the rest of the muck coating your body."

Now what? It wasn't as nasty a shock as discovering the smashed egg, or that Sammy Jo was a time-traveller, but nevertheless, he was utterly winded at losing the camouflage of filth that had built up over the long decades of neglect since Ekaterraina had deserted him. No more would he be able to stretch out against the rock walls on the sunning terrace and doze, completely ignored by other dragons, while they basked and gossiped... No more would he be able to come and go, beneath the notice of the Overlord and his cronies...

Sammy Jo looked up at him with huge hurt eyes. "D-don't you *like* it, Granddad? When I rubbed – and saw the lovely shine underneath, I th-thought you'd be *so* pleased to look so *lovely*..." she broke off, evidently overcome.

"Yes, yes," he babbled, desperate to head off any tears. "It's a shock, that's all. Waking up to find myself looking so different."

"I'll bet!" snorted Rondell, muttering in an undertone that wasn't nearly quiet enough, "Pity you didn't drop dead with the surprise."

He threw his son-in-law a slitted glance. *Make the most of your disrespectful comments, you scrawny excuse for a lord. Because by the time we've finished cleaning me up, you'll be fawning at my feet!*

Emmy Lou burst into noisy tears. "C-can't believe you s-said s-such a nasty thing to my D-dad!" she sobbed.

"Oh, don't cry, Mummy!" Sammy Jo swarmed up her mother's leg and neck, covering her emerald scales with flickering licks and loving steam. "Daddy was just making one of his jokes. He really *loves* it that Granddad is here..." Those searchlight eyes of hers swung an imploring look across to Rondell, "Don't you, Daddy?"

"Hey, babe, didn't mean it! You know me – singeing my own foot, every time I open my mouth," jabbered that waste of skin and scales, edging towards the door.

Which was exactly what Castellan yearned to do. "There, there..." He awkwardly extended his tongue, brushing his daughter's brow-ridge. Then winced as she crashed against his sore, stiff body, still bawling.

"He's just a flame-brained male," he stuttered, "We're good for mating flights... hunting food... guarding territory. Everything else – including keeping peace in our own aery – not so much."

"I'll... go check on the egg," mumbled Rondell, scooting out of the guest chamber.

At once, Emmy Lou ceased crying and straightened up, fixing him with *that* look. "When you're all cleaned up – you give your word that you won't crisp him. And I'm after a solid Vow, not some half-hearted maybe," she gabbled, in a sub-sonic whisper. "I know he's not the brightest, but he's not as stupid as you think. It's just you make him nervous, so he says the first flea-witted thing that floats into his head. But he's a constant mate, a nearly reasonable provider, and usually a kind father. In short – he's the best Wyvern Peak, or anywhere else for that matter, has to offer."

He opened his mouth to deny that he'd ever

considered the notion. And shut it, again. It was pointless lying to Emmy Lou, she was far too like her mother. "He's not my choice for you," he said, finally. "But so long as he – mostly – makes you happy, then I'll let him be."

"He mostly does," said Emmy Lou. "And now I'd better check on the egg. Make sure he's not got some hazy notion of trying to bond with our son before he's hatched." She scooped up her daughter, bringing Sammy Jo level with her own swirling eyes. "And the reason I'm letting you witness this, is because you need to know that being a successful queen isn't always about being tough. And to test whether you can keep this chat a secret. Because if you can't – I shan't be giving you any more such lessons. Understood?"

"Yes, Mummy," whispered Sammy Jo, her wings hanging submissively as her mother plonked her onto the ground.

"Good." Emmy Lou swept out of the guest chamber without a backward look.

Sammy Jo gazed up at him and put her foreleg to her mouth in a silent, "Shh."

He froze, straining his ears for the tell-tale click of talons on stones, or rasp of scale on scale. After a tense, breath-held moment, they both relaxed.

"Mummy sometimes likes to act as if she's gone, when she's only crept around the corner to listen," confided Sammy Jo.

"I know," he said, grimly. "She caught the habit from your Grandma." He frowned down at the dragonet, whose submissive pose was now gone, he noticed. "Here's a stake-lined pit, and no mistake! I'm guessing you've got some kind of answer to this business of cleaning me up. Because unless you were scrubbing my scales all night, you couldn't possibly have produced that shine."

Her gaze widened. "How did you *know*? Mummy and Daddy didn't."

He snorted. "My scales, remember? I know just how much effort it takes to get them spotless and keep them that way. It's one of the main reasons why I decided it wasn't worth the bother, anymore." *And I was too broken-hearted to care.*

"When you warmed up and you were sleeping – your snoring was shaking the mud from your scales as they steamed. All I had to do, was give them a quick polish and they sparkled." She hopped around, her small crest flicking. "It was fun!"

It made sense that steaming them would shift the dirt. He sighed. "Pity I wasn't awake at the time. Together we could probably have managed to get a lot more off."

"That's exactly what I was thinking!" Sammy Jo patted his foot fondly with her tongue. "I really like it when we get the same idea at the same time. Normally it's me and Billy Bob that think together, like that."

"Hm." He wasn't quite sure exactly which idea they'd had at the same time, so stayed quiet, hoping she'd reveal their joint brainwave sometime soon.

"We'll have to wait till everyone's gone, of course," she added.

"Of course." He decided to stay put in the guest chamber, while Emmy Lou set about organising Rondell and Billy Bob, who'd woken up peevish and weepy on account of missing Sammy Jo.

He'd expected her to rush to comfort him, as her small brother wailed for her.

But though she sighed a couple of times, Sammy Jo started scratching out a chess board in the dirt, instead. "I'm being punished. And anyhow, I'm not always going to be there to keep his wings straight. Especially when the new hatchling comes along. So it's time he got used to not having me always there.

"Do you want to play with the smooth or jagged side, Granddad?"

There'd been one tricky moment, when Emmy Lou attempted to sneak up on them – but fortunately Sammy Jo's keen young ears picked up a noise and she quickly snatched up the Jagged Overlord and started scratching away at a dirt-crusted scale on his flank.

"We're leaving now." Emmy Lou bounded into the guest chamber. "You haven't got very far, have you?" she said smugly.

"Living alongside that waste of skin and scales hasn't improved your manners, I see!" He wasn't having to act very hard to appear thoroughly annoyed at her rude interruption.

"I hope you're not going to leave Sammy Jo to do it all on her own, Father. Where's your polishing sand? Or rubbing sticks?"

He glared at her, smoke trickling from his nostrils. "Do I *look* as if I own a tub of polishing sand or rubbing sticks?"

She muttered something under her breath – he hated it when females did that – and then rushed off, returning a few moments later with a stack of tubs and an armful of fray-ended sticks. "There. I'll get more supplies rounded up later. Bye then." She eyed them both suspiciously. "And behave!"

"Yes, Mummy. Bye."

"Why wouldn't we?" he snapped.

"I was talking to Sammy Jo as it happens." Emmy Lou smirked, before whisking through the door too fast to allow him to have the last word.

Another typical female trick he hated.

"Now we can get going!" announced Sammy Jo, dancing on her talon-tips in excitement, looking at him expectantly.

"Hm." Fortunately, he'd had plenty of practice over the years of appearing to know more than he did, it being a major skill of dragon lords.

She frowned. "How do you start? Last night, you sort of leapt forward, but stayed in one place..."

It finally dawned on him. "You want us to time-travel to get me clean?"

"Yes! The muck just drops off when you're all steamy." She was right. No doubt about it, it would save hours, if not days, of grinding effort.

However... "I made a promise never to travel through time, again," he said, heavily.

"But you're not *going* anywhere. So it can't be travelling, can it?" Sammy Jo stretched her neck in that way of hers. "You're getting yourself clean. And showing me how to go time-sliding. So I don't have to try it all on my own."

"No! It's far too dangerous for a dragonet of your size to go time-sliding— I mean, time-travelling alone." He shuddered, dread trickling through to his wingtips. "Don't you dare try it on your own! There's a dozen accidents waiting to happen – and no one to come and rescue you."

"Except you, Granddad. You'd come and get me, wouldn't you?" She looked up at him. Trust, terrible and crushing, shone out of those huge eyes and he realised he was beaten.

*

They had just returned from their third sortie over frozen minutes and seconds when he realised two things. The first was he was ravenous. The second – he was running out of energy. Time-travel, especially short distances where he couldn't simply stretch his wings and fly over frozen year hills and ice decades, was exhausting.

It was doing the trick, though. As his ice-covered scales steamed, it merely took some knocks, along with a couple of rolls to loosen off the layers of muck and a few wipes with the stuff the food used to cover themselves up with – nasty indigestible stuff. Though it mopped up moisture and stray clods of mud well enough. It was mostly his tail and wings now still coated with years of grime. Other than that, he glittered. His ebony-coloured scales nicely set off his battle honours – the metal he'd ingested, along with the food he'd consumed, grew in sparkling streaks that toughened the scales plating his body. In fact there was so much metal, he realised with something of a shock, a number of smaller scales along his neck and belly were mostly gold, silver and that hard tin the food used as armour. No wonder moving around and flying was getting so difficult!

Sammy Jo became increasingly thrilled as the extent of his glory was uncovered, bit by bit. Inevitably, some of the precious metal was knocked out, along with the dirt, as his long-neglected scales all needed trimming back, anyway.

He nudged a small pile of the golden and silver shards towards Sammy Jo. "Go on, miss. Time you put a bit of shine on."

"For me?" she breathed, her eyes widening.

He nodded, a bit shaken at how grateful he was that they were taking a break from their mini-hops into the past. "Maybe you could collect up the rest of the treasure for Mummy," he added, gesturing to the piles of dirt.

Sammy Jo's grateful gaze melted parts of his shrivelled old heart he'd thought forever frozen, as she started nudging at the small pile of gold and silver fragments with her nose. And opening her mouth...

"Not like that!" he yelped, appalled at her ignorance. "You mustn't eat cold metal – not at your age. It's always better molten, anyway." He took a breath, rolled the air around his mouth before sucking it down into his flame sac, and released a small firestorm that reduced the pile of gold to a hissing puddle.

He watched her lap it up, noting with approval that for all her greedy eagerness, she didn't waste a drop.

"Mm..." She finally looked up when the stone floor was licked clean. "That was *lovely*, Granddad. Now, shall we go time-sliding again?"

With a sinking heart, he realised that while he'd merely had a chance to rest up, Sammy Jo was fizzing with newfound energy, courtesy of her metallic snack.

"What'd you say to travelling back a bit further?"

"Oh, yes!" She bounced around on her talon-tips, wings unfurling with excitement.

He scowled down at her. "But you do exactly as you're told! None of your awkward questions and answering back while we're on the wing, is that clear?"

"Oh! We're *flying*…" she breathed.

"*I'm* flying. You'll be tucked onto my back, hanging onto my crest as if your life depends on it. Because it does! It'll be colder up there and if you're too small to keep your furnace going – and you are – then it'll go out. And you'll die." He allowed wisps of smoke to trickle out of his nose, hoping she'd assume anger was causing it, rather than gritted fear. "Only reason I'm taking you at all, is that I don't trust you not to go plunging off alone while I'm gone."

Because that's exactly what I'd have done when I was your age… "And you're too small! Even frozen minutes and seconds can swallow you up. I was at least twice your size when I started time travelling. So you hang on, miss! Just because I managed to save your unborn brother doesn't mean I could necessarily go back and save you. Understand?"

"Yes, Granddad," whispered Sammy Jo, flattened onto the ground, her wings completely slack.

Ah… so that's what she looks like when properly submissive! He realised that he hadn't seen her that way, even when Rondell was struggling not to flame the pair of them after smashing the egg. *She's fond of him, but doesn't respect him.* Which was dangerous. As a lord, he was capable of killing her in a fit of rage. *What's Emmy Lou thinking, to allow such a state of affairs to occur?* As he gruffly ordered the small dragon aboard, he reflected that it was just as well he'd returned to Wyvern Peak when he had. Because with the extra strain of raising and hatching another egg with only two adults in their family cluster, there could so easily be a nasty accident. And it wouldn't be young Billy Bob who'd draw down his father's rage, but this little miss, with her impertinent questions.

He took his time making sure she was properly tucked in under his crest, protected by the chilly air that would be whistling past her and yet still with a good view of the ground. He was gratified that at least she seemed thoroughly familiar with the drill of flying on the back of an adult. Though he'd only really know once he was on the wing and it was too late to do much about it. As he stretched his neck and sucked in a huge lungful to fire up his furnace, a thrill of anticipation ran through him. A stirring of fearful excitement that he hadn't felt for so long, he'd almost forgotten the sensation. How *alive* it made everything seem. How sharp and precious!

He leapt. Spreading his tattered wings, feeling the tug and pull of the frigid air as he clawed minutes and seconds into hummocks of hours. Two… three… four… He'd forgotten how beautiful they'd looked from up here. How free and *powerful* he felt when flying back through Time.

"Whee!" Sammy Jo bugled from his back, clinging on tightly.

Five… They'd have to turn back very soon – she was too small to be able to—

What's that? A shadow passed over the top of them. Something big. Flying. He peered up, straining to see through the misty air.

Another dragon! Fear zipped through him as he got a fleeting sense of her determination – for it was a queen.

Her longing and loneliness…

"Hold tight!" he trumpeted as he felt Sammy Jo's grip shift. She was clearly peering upwards, judging by the way her body shape had altered across his neck. And he plunged into a tight turn, diving back down for Wyvern Peak. He'd also got the sense that she'd been up there for a while, looking… Chances were, she'd missed the fact they'd entered so quickly and wouldn't be expecting them to leave so fast. That's what he was hoping.

They'd be returning some three hours further into the future, he realised, but that couldn't be helped. Better that, than risk being attacked in mid-air while encumbered by the child.

The queen called. A desperate sound.

Hah! She can't find us. Thank the Great Roarer we've shaken her off.

And just as he gritted his teeth and started the agonising race back to the present, Sammy Jo squalled. A high piercing scream.

What's she playing at? She'll bring the queen right to our doorstep!

He was so shocked, he nearly cannoned into a melting hummock of minutes. It was a struggle to keep his balance. Now would *not* be a good time to crash land – not with young missy on board. Though it would serve her right if he dumped her into that pool of seconds. Right there!

Ahh! It *hurt*! Though the pain definitely wasn't as great as it had been last night. Another detail he'd forgotten. The more he travelled, the less returning had bothered him. Another flick of his wings – and he'd be down. Though if he was going to make a habit of this, he'd definitely need to shed more metal, he was really too heavy for these manoeuvres...

These thoughts and a dozen more streamed through his head as he lined up his position. Waking up his dormant senses as his body responded to the demands of an emergency landing. While a large part of him was shaking with the shock of what might have happened if that half-mad queen had caught them on the wing, his *wild* part wanted to bugle in triumph that they'd returned safely.

Because, here they were. Returned. In the guest chamber at Wyvern Peak. He back-winged, conscious of his small passenger and knowing it would have to be the smoothest of smooth landings. Allowing his claws to trail in the flowing time-stream, slowing down the minutes and selecting the second when they'd pop back in. Now!

Just before he fully arrived, he sensed a *wrongness*. And if it hadn't been for that wretched queen cris-crossing the skies evidently waiting for them, he'd have spun round right then and there and taken off again.

And then he couldn't. Something was flung over him. A net. Which pressed against his scales and *hurt*.

Sammy Jo! She'll be crushed...

He roared his outrage and fury through clamped lips, which – somehow – wouldn't open. *Magic!* He *hated* the tricky stuff. Along with the nasty creatures that used it. Sure enough, standing in front of him were those cursed dwarves.

Their Overlord – may all his children be hatched with wooden legs – was standing right in the middle of the guest chamber, his arms folded, his ugly hairy face creased into a scowl.

Two things immediately occurred to him – the first was that this coterie of dwarf warriors needed to have had Wendell Bo's permission to be right in the heart of Wyvern Peak. And the second was that still wouldn't have cut any ice with Emmy Lou. He tried rearing up. And squalled as the net tightened in agonising bands around his body.

The dwarf overlord tapped him on the nose.

He shook with fury, fighting the magic binding his jaws shut.

"No point in struggling, Castellan," jeered the unspeakable creature. "We have your real name. And we have a strong mage, so you better settle down and listen. This is all your own fault. You broke your word. You promised never to go time travelling again. And yet, there you were. Up to your old tricks."

He took a couple of deep breaths and forced down his dragon instincts. This was a situation that called for cool thinking. He blinked his eyes slowly and shook his head from side to side. *I'm not admitting to anything while you have me gagged...*

"So, you want to Parley?" the dwarf enquired, baring his brown teeth in a nasty smile.

He fantasised about flaming his smug face so it melted off his ugly monkey skull. Which was when he felt Sammy Jo shift and move under his crest, and he realised that she'd somehow escaped being crushed by the magical cords that made up the net.

She's still alive!

He recalled the dwarves used a nodding motion to

show when they agreed with something, so he wagged his head up and down. Twice.

The dwarf's toothy snarl got wider as he waved at one of his warriors, his impertinent, mocking gaze never leaving his eyes. "How does it feel, Oath-breaker, to know there are those here in your aery who would see the back of you, such that they'd betray you?"

Six. There were six of them. Five with weapons, and one staring at him with a fixed look, mumbling, looking as if he was trying to pass an egg. They stabbed at him with their spears, not hard enough to pierce his face scales, but hard enough to hurt. One hairy wretch jabbed him so close to his right eye with his spear butt, that he had to jerk to avoid the risk of being blinded. Dizzy with the agony of the net biting into his scales, binding his mouth so tightly that his teeth were slicing his own lips, it was the humiliation that pained him most. Using the indignity as a focus, he forced himself to think, rather than react.

They are trying to enrage me such that I cannot think or reason. And in any case, struggling to free myself isn't working. So if I continue, I'll risk further injuring myself. And endangering Sammy Jo. So he pushed his fury into a small corner of his mind. And slumped, as if in the throes of defeat.

The net around his mouth suddenly slackened, allowing him to suck in a lungful of air. He panted, as if he was at the end of his strength, while sucking in several more lungfuls of air, feeling it expand on the way down, firing his furnace.

Which was when, behind him, little Sammy Jo jumped across to the wall he was backed against. He heard her slither down without making too much noise, still hidden behind his body. While desperately hoping she hadn't been damaged by the magic net that had snared him.

To distract these horrible creatures, he sighed. "I want to Parley. So lend me your name as I once parleyed with your fathers." The dwarfish words were rough-edged and awkward in his mouth. It had been a long, long time since he'd spoken their ugly language.

"Call me Cheldric. Do you deny you were time-travelling?" demanded the nasty creature, whose name was definitely not Cheldric.

He could hear the drone of one of Wendell Bo's cronies – Silas Jed, if he wasn't mistaken – translating to the dragonkin congregated outside the aery. He could smell and hear there were at least two-score of them, other than his own horrified family cluster. And felt a surge of contempt that they'd allow the dwarves to march in and mistreat one of their own kind. Such a thing would never have happened back when dragonkin truly ruled the skies.

"Yes. I absolutely deny I was time-travelling!" he said in dwarfish, repeating it in dragonese to make sure everyone knew of his innocence. "I slipped back a matter of moments in order to clean my scales. At no time did I re-emerge, or do anything to change the time-stream. Apart from a small incident last night when an egg got accidentally broken. And even that was entirely a domestic matter involving a mere clawful of minutes."

He could feel Sammy Jo's body pressing against his flank, trembling.

"Aha! So you admit to changing the time-stream!"

Not-Cheldric pointed a finger at him.

"For the sake of an egg. Within my own dwelling," he protested. "Surely you wouldn't begrudge a grandfather the joy of seeing another hatchling? It hardly constitutes changing the time-stream!" He repeated his words in dragonese to ensure that everyone heard the correct version.

Not-Cheldric put his hands on his hips, shouting, "But where's it going to end. Eh? So you make up some tale about saving an egg. The next day you're diving in and out of the time-stream, cleaning yourself up. For what? A leadership challenge? And then what? You'll rekindle your feud with the dwarves and our human cousins?"

Ah. So you've made a peace treaty with the food— humans, have you? That's worth knowing.

He sagged to the ground, allowing his utter exhaustion to suffuse his voice, "I'm old. Older than any dragon alive here. I made my oath not to change the time-stream to your forefathers over two hundred years ago. Surely if I'd entertained ambitions to become Overlord, I wouldn't have waited until I was so elderly and infirm."

Not-Cheldric looked around at his followers. "Oh yes! We saw just how old and feeble you were when you first appeared!" He jabbed him impudently in the face with the butt of his spear.

He *ached* to snatch at the wretched stick, pulling the creature within range of his mouth, so he could rip his sorry head off. But Sammy Jo was still hiding behind him. And if he put up any resistance, resulting in being further hurt, he felt sickly certain the dragonet would rush out and attack, heedless of her safety.

So he gritted his teeth, forcing his head to flop onto the floor, before answering in a dragging croak, "Of course I did! A group of strangers are in my dwelling, threatening my family. What would you do in my place? Try to protect them, of course. But…" he sighed. "I'm old and sick. I came back here to spend time with my grandchildren before I die. And… as you can see, I am easy to vanquish. In my prime, you would never have held me. Even with your magic."

"For shame! We allow these mud-diggers to come into our aery to make war on our elderly," bugled Emmy Lou from the entrance.

He could feel Sammy Jo bunching, getting ready. Before he could say or do anything, she shot out from behind him, leaping forward, scrabbling frantically. She froze in mid-air for a long second, while her small scales started icing over. And then disappeared with a small popping noise.

"What was that?" demanded Not-Cheldric, grasping his sword and looking around.

"Another time-traveller. A dragonet!" shrieked the mage, a skinny creature. "And it's escaped."

Not-Cheldric's nasty skin turned a vile blotched red as he jabbed his spear at his throat. "Did you know that wormling?" he demanded.

The net slithered and tightened, compelling him to tell the truth. "Of course I did. She's my granddaughter."

"And did you know she could do that – travel back through time?" he demanded.

"No. I didn't," He replied, startled that she had managed to escape into the Timescape unaided. *Oh,*

Sammy Jo, what have you done? If you stay there, you'll die of cold. And if you come back, they'll take you with them. She must have panicked, of course she did, poor little wormling!

Sure enough, less than two minutes later, a soft popping sound in the exact space where she'd disappeared, announced her reappearance.

Given the stress of the situation, the fact that she managed to return with such precision without any help just underlined her amazing raw talent. Though he wasn't sure if she wouldn't have been better off dying in the frozen hinterland, rather than back here...

She didn't even get a chance to land. Greedy digger hands snatched her out of the air.

The skinny mage crushed her to him. "Well, look at this. We have our very own time-travelling dragon now!" He put his face close to hers. "Once we've tamed it, we'll be invincible," he gloated.

Sammy Jo seemed to melt into the creature's arms, going boneless. As if overcome with fear. Or... She shot him a slitted glance, slightly tilting her head and twitched one wing.

He sucked in a slow, deep breath, not daring to hope that such a youngling could be so resourceful.

Not-Cheldric bared his teeth in a triumphant snarl. "We'll be on our way. And to ensure you don't go on any more jaunts, we'll take this little one with us. Don't worry, she'll be very well looked after—"

Sammy Jo erupted into a whirling flurry of snapping teeth and flashing claws – and the mage, yelping, stumbled.

The magical bands imprisoning him slackened off –

not completely – but then, they didn't have to. He surged up, then hesitated, gritting his teeth at their biting pain.

Which was when the green queen, who'd been hunting them earlier, erupted into the room. Right behind the mage, still struggling with Sammy Jo. She was magnificent. Or would have been if she wasn't so skinny and cris-crossed with terrible scars. But the moment she saw Sammy Jo, she popped back out of existence.

The scene melted…

And reformed, once more. Another timestream.

He didn't have time to be terrified at the consequences of two timestreams colliding. Because the horrible dwarven creature had just grabbed Sammy Jo out of the air, again, crushing her to him. "Well, look at this. We have our very own time-travelling dragon now!" He put his face close to hers, gloating, "Once we've tamed it, we'll be invincible."

Sammy Jo seemed to melt into the creature's arms, going boneless. As if overcome with fear. Or… She shot him a slitted glance, slightly tilting her head and twitched one wing.

He sucked in a slow, deep breath, determined to save her this time around.

Once again, Not-Cheldric bared his rotten teeth. "We'll be on our way. And to ensure you don't go on any more jaunts, we'll take this little one with us. Don't worry, she'll be very well looked after—"

Sammy Jo erupted into a whirling flurry of snapping teeth and flashing claws – and the mage, yelping, stumbled.

The magical bands imprisoning him slackened off.

This time around, he surged towards the mage, heedless of the pain. The mage jumped back with a yelp, losing his grip on Sammy Jo, who fought free with a frantic scrabble of wings and claws, allowing her to pop into nothingness, once more.

He barely had time to feel relieved triumph at being able to save Sammy Jo, when the green queen, who'd been hunting them earlier, erupted into the room. Right behind the mage, still stumbling and cursing after having lost Sammy Jo.

The queen was magnificent. Or would have been if she wasn't so skinny and cris-crossed with terrible scars. Which didn't stop her grabbing the mage's head and shoulders in her mouth. The creature writhed, his legs waggling as blood leaked and squirted, before disappearing down her gullet. As she burped, happily, the magical net abruptly fizzed into nothingness, freeing him.

He had a fleeting glimpse of Not-Cheldric staring at him, his eyes wide and his mouth stretched in fear, arms flung up.

Before a gout of flame poured from his mouth. The creature didn't even have time to scream.

"Granddad?" said the queen, staring across at him.

And suddenly it fell into place. Made horrible, terrible sense…

He realised there must have been a time-stream when Sammy Jo didn't escape. When the dwarves made off with her, believing they could bend her into obedience and turn her into a time-travelling slave. But this was Sammy Jo, who didn't bend to anyone. So they'd starved her and wrapped her in magical netting until they'd cris-crossed her beautiful scales with scars. Until, somehow, years later and nearly full-grown, she'd escaped and went back to the last place where she'd been happy, to change her terrible fate. She'd been looking for them, earlier. Not to attack, but to mark the exact spot where she'd need to enter, ready to kill her chief tormentor.

No wonder the young Sammy Jo riding on his back had called to her! Some instinct would have told her this battered, desperate queen wasn't any enemy, but someone needing help. Her help.

He folded his wings around his now-grown granddaughter. "Oh, Kindling..."

"The time-stream before – they killed you," her voice was muffled. "While you were still trapped in the net, they chopped your head off. Then took me with them. Told me later it was because they knew you'd never give up searching for me. So it was my fault. That's why I came back. To put it right."

He stepped back, looking around. The scene was frozen. Of course it was. It had to be, given that Sammy Jo had crossed two time-streams – something he'd been told never to do – in order for her older self to help free him. And now, somehow they'd slipped sideways out of that time-stream. If they hadn't, there would have been another terrible explosion, like the one in Devastation Valley and Wyvern Peak would be no more... Except—

"Don't worry." Sammy Jo flicked her crest as she looked around the frozen timescape.

Not-Cheldric, scorched, though not fully cooked, was caught mid-way in the act of falling to the floor, deader than last night's supper. The other dwarves were stuck in various attitudes of panic. One had lunged toward him with his horrible spear. He took great pleasure in plucking it out of the creature's hands and splintering it into kindling.

"I *pulled* us here." continued Sammy Jo, as if such a feat was an everyday occurrence. "I know what happens when one time-stream gets swallowed by another. If you stay in the present it's a terrible mess, but here… That's why it's so cold. It stops the different time-streams exploding when they touch each other."

He stared at the frost riming everything, his breath pluming from his mouth in a fountain of ice crystals. "So that's why everything is frozen." All these years and he'd never known why. Because neither had Grimwurt.

And if I had, then maybe I could have avoided the tragedy of Devastation Valley… Though he'd spent too long picking over the carcass of that regret, he realised. It was past time he moved on, given too many years and time streams had grown from that event to be able to go back and undo it, now. And with that realisation, the guilt-laden boulder pressing on his heart for all these years, rolled away. He'd still always grieve for all those fine warrior lords who'd been lost – but no longer would he be buckled under the crushing sense that it was all his fault. *I didn't know…*

"When they weren't punishing me, their magic-twister taught me a lot. More than he knew, actually." She was changing in front of his eyes. Bulking out and blooming into a dazzling beauty, sufficient to rival her mother. In between one smoking breath and another, the terrible scars deforming and twisting her scales faded, then were gone. Her eyes gleamed with energy and health, as the consequences of her terrible past were swallowed up and turning into another, happier fate.

"Oh, and Granddad – remember you told me about how if everyone knew we could time-travel, they could snatch Mummy or Billy Bob to hold as hostage?" her adult voice had deepened, sounding eerily like Ekaterraina in her prime.

"Hm." He was mesmerised by the sight and sound of her. While haunted by the memory of what those hairy fiends would have done to her, had they succeeded in kidnapping her…

"Well, I've worked it out. If there's two of us, unless they kill us at exactly the same time, they don't stand a chance. One of us can always jump into the Time-World to rescue Mummy and Billy Bob, while unravelling their plot." Her voice became a snarl as her eyes slitted. "And return to slaughter them!"

She's right. Of course she is. Just so long as I live long enough to see her fully grown again. Which he could do, easily. It was only ever a question of wanting to.

"C-c-cold…" came a small voice from behind the scorched dwarf, now covered in a rime of frost. "Want din-dins…"

"Bills!" As she uttered the words, scooping up her baby brother, it seemed impossible to Castellan that he hadn't immediately realised this was Sammy Jo all grown up. "Ooo… you're going to grow up to time-travel too! We'll be able to fly around here together. It's going to be *lovely*! I'm so looking forward to it." Her tongue flicked out and gently stroked his brow-ridge, before she turned to him, handing Billy Bob across.

"Good-bye, Granddad. Thank you for taking care of me."

"What'll happen?" he blinked. "Will you be stuck here forever?"

"Oh no. I'll hop across to the time-stream where I escaped as dragonet, then pop back some six minutes and seventeen seconds later, once you and me have vanquished those dwarves."

"So next time I'll see you, you'll be that pesky little nuisance, again." He didn't want to leave. He wanted to stand here for another dozen years staring at the beautiful, brave dragon she'd grown into. But Billy Bob stirred, shivering and fretful. "Better return him. I've no idea how he got here in the first place."

"I know! Isn't he clever?" Sammy Jo's grin sparkled. "So you'd better get him back before he freezes."

"Hm. And now I'll have two of you to keep out've trouble while time-travelling." He sighed. "Pesky lizards, the pair of you." He wheeled round and raced back to Wyvern Peak, smugly satisfied that for once, he was the one who'd had the last word.

Getting back wasn't nearly the struggle he'd expected. Indeed, while it wasn't exactly easy – he wasn't enough of a fool to treat it with such a lack of respect – it wasn't all that hard, either. Clearly, he was getting back into the swing of time-travelling far faster than he could have possibly hoped. Just as well, really.

IV – Not-So Picky Eaters...

He'd popped back into the main chamber of Rondell's lair, just as Not-Cheldric thumped onto the floor, burnt and crispy. The other dwarves were staring up at him with fear-stretched eyes, mouths opening...

Time to put an end to them. He knew from experience that they'd make a terrible noise once they started bellowing. And he didn't want their noise to frighten little Billy Bob, who was bouncing in his grasp, squeaking, "Din-dins! Wan' more din-dins!"

A gout of white-hot flame soon put paid to any trouble they were thinking of causing – as well as igniting all that hair they were afflicted with, both on the tops and the bottoms of their heads. Which pleased him, because nothing tasted worse than half-singed dwarven hair – not even part-cooked sheep's wool.

This was when Sammy Jo popped back into the chamber with a scutter of frosted wings and claws, small and innocent. And free of the memory of what those vile dwarves would have done to her, had they succeeded in capturing her.

It was he who plucked her out of the air, this time around. Far more gently than that cursed mage. "Greetings, Kindling. We have prevailed," he announced. As if she were a fellow warrior. *Which she is, in another time-stream...*

Best not to think about such things too much. Old Grimwurt had advised against it, claiming that if time-travellers got to worrying about how time-streams criscrossed each other, at best they'd get a nasty headache. And at worst it could turn them mad. Grimwurt had claimed that poor Thudbane had ended up trying to fly to the Sun, after believing it was a ball of exploding gas that would keep dragon furnaces burning forever, if only he could reach it. A load of nonsense! Because everyone knew the Sun was Old Roarer, himself, the biggest dragon the world had ever seen, having exploded after trying to melt the snow-caps.

"Granddad?" chirped Sammy Jo. "Are you alright? Your eyes are crossing."

He blinked, realising he was just about to fall into the stake-lined trap that Grimwurt had warned him against.

The aroma of cooked dwarf filled his nostrils, so he carefully picked off two morsels, and was offering them to the dragonets, when a scuffling stampede burst into the chamber, headed by Emmy Lou, and closely followed by Rondell, tripping over her tail. While Wendell Bo and his three heavies barged in, after pushing their way to the front of the rest of the crowd pouring through the entrance.

He put the children down behind him, starting to straighten up.

Then saw the aggressive gleam in Wendell Bo's eyes.

And slumped. *I'm not in any fit state to take on Wendell and his cronies. Yet. And if I did – do I want the job of overlording this pestiferous place? Absolutely not. I'm going to be far too busy training Sammy Jo and Billy Bob.*

He sighed. It would have to be Plan Three, then. Because while Plan One was to fight and overthrow Wendell and his cronies, and Plan Two was to convince the rest of the aery to overthrow Wendell Bo, Plan Three was...

He sagged, staggering a little. "Thank goodness, you've arrived. I don't feel... Oh... dear little Sammy Jo, here was able to flame the last dwarf for me, didn't you, child?"

Emmy Lou had scooped up Billy Bob, ignoring his indignant cries for more din-dins.

While Sammy Jo had fluttered up to perch on Castellan's crest. Probably because she'd seen the look, part relief and part baffled fury, on her mother's face.

Wendell Bo shoved Rondell out of the way, though he sidestepped around Emmy Lou, Castellan noticed, coming to stop right in front of him.

"They won't like it!" he declared in that reedy shrill of his. "They won't like it one little bit."

He looked at the dragonets, who were still chewing the roasted dwarf with enthusiasm. "Oh, I think they do, Overlord."

Wendell glared up at him. "I wasn't talking about the food! I'm talking about the dwarves – they won't like it."

He tried to shrink down so he was eye to eye with the Overlord, even though it was killing his back to do so.

"Let's hope not, Sire. We crisped them enough so they shouldn't like anything ever again."

Wendell Bo sucked in a long breath, evidently trying to make himself taller and bulkier than Castellan, teetering on tip-talons and puffing up his crest till it looked ready to burst. The effect was ruined when he overbalanced, falling off his tippy-talons and cannoning into the bulk of Silas Jed, hulking at his side.

"Stop crowding me, you maggot-brained mealworm!" he snapped to his underling.

Whose eyes kindled amber, he was interested to see, before, with a visible effort, the sidekick controlled his temper. "Apologies, Overlord."

He took advantage of the distraction to slump onto his haunches, and straighten his poor kinked spine, which probably would never be the same again.

Silas Jed decided to pass the pain along. "You sitting in the presence of your Overlord, you black streak of uselessness?"

"My pardon, Sire. It's been a hard day. And these old bones aren't what they were. No disrespect intended, Overlord," he quavered, trying to flatten his crest still further. Though it, too, was protesting at being pushed into such an unfamiliar shape. *That's the trouble with this old body of mine – it's sadly out of practice. Can't recall when I last had to cringe in submission to anything, or anyone.*

Which was when Sammy Jo scrambled across to his shoulder and flattened her wings beautifully in submission. "'Cuse me, Overlord." The effect was slightly spoilt by the fact she was talking around a mouthful of roasted dwarf. "My Granddad is really, really old. Mummy says we have to be kind to him. On account of his decrep— decrep-it-ude." She looked across to Emmy Lou, wide-eyed and earnest. "Is that the right word, Mummy?"

What! Emmy Lou said that? His mind was spinning with outrage – until he registered Emmy Lou's sharp exhale. It was his daughter's tell when she was caught flat-winged and unprepared. And the reason he knew it so well, was because it hardly ever happened.

"That's right, Kindling. Though…" Her glance to him was genuinely apologetic. "He used to be a great warrior, remember. We don't want to hurt his feelings."

His cue. "That's alright…" He broke off to cough weakly. "Those days are so very long ago, it's a wonder that anyone remembers them.. "

"Some of us don't!"

He ignored Rondell's comment, to push his point home. Wendell Bo was clearly too dim to appreciate subtlety. "As I said, when you kindly allowed me permission to stay here with my family – I just want to live out the sunset of my life, sunning my old bones and maybe doing a spot of babysitting."

"Quite. Though I don't recall you mentioning any time travelling. Or bringing dwarves to our aery." Wendell looked down at the remaining dwarven pieces on the floor, peevishly. "They won't like it, you know."

"Allow me, Overlord…" He selected a nicely crisped thigh, flicking away the charred covering. And as he swung round, he snapped off one of the longer, golden scales protruding from his belly and placed it on top of the meat. "I hear it's a hazardous journey from the lands of their burrows – mines, I think they call them, to this, our aery. Up long winding roads. I hear dwarves don't have a head for heights." He gently flamed the joint, heating it through and melting the gold, till it ran across the flesh in a glistening sauce. He placed it in front of the greedy fool. "What a shame they never arrived."

Wendell Bo's eyes closed in pure pleasure as his mouth closed upon the meat. "Mm... Didn't know they tasted so good!"

"And you, Sire – would you care for a piece of... sheep," he asked Silas Jed.

"What sheep? It's not sheep, it's—" Wendell Bo broke off with a laugh, as he at long last caught up. He gestured towards Castellan's kills magnanimously. "Share them out. Let's have a feast!"

So they did. He hunched against the wall, watching Wendell Bo act the generous host, as dragons lined up for smaller and smaller helpings of dwarf – doled out by Rondell and Emmy Lou – until all that was left were teeth. And no one wanted those, mostly because the majority were black and rotten.

Plan Three had worked. He'd abased himself sufficiently, so that Wendell Bo was convinced he wouldn't be a threat to his rule as Overlord. Castellan of old would have rather died than suffer such indignity. But then, Castellan of old hadn't had to consider the needs of two pesky lizards.

By the time everyone had left, it was nearly time for the dragonet's bedtime. But of course, they were hungry again. After all, they hadn't had very much to eat, before that slack-winged idiot they called a leader, had given it all away.

Then he had an idea. There was a place where five dwarves still existed. True, they were a tad frozen – but he was sure the journey forward in time would nicely thaw them out...

*

Some time later, the family were lolling in the chamber, contentedly full.

"That was scrummy." sighed Sammy Jo, slumped against his side. "Lovely and free-range."

Emmy Lou, leaning against Rondell, shot her daughter a sharp look. "I wouldn't mention free-range food in front of Granddad, if I were you. Especially as you spent a whole day on the naughty crag, because you wouldn't say sorry!"

"Still not sorry. Cos if I hadn't done it, Granddad wouldn't be here. And having Granddad here is flaming brilliant," announced Sammy Jo, stretching her neck in that female way of hers.

"Mind your manners when you're talking to your mother!" he growled, smoke wisping from his nostrils.

She flattened her wings in full submission. "Sorry, Granddad."

Emmy Lou's exclamation was a mixture of resentment and admiration. "Gah! How have you got the measure of her so fast? We've tried everything to get proper respect from her."

He shrugged. "Practice. Your mother and I were landed with you. She's not so different." *Uncannily alike, as it happens...* He stretched, then got to his feet. "Come on, scatterlings, let's get you ready for a good long nap."

"Don't wanna nap!" whined Billy Bob, as he hustled

them off to the nursery.

"It's fine, Bills." Sammy Jo ambled up to her little brother and draped her foreleg around his neck. "You be good and once you're on your sleeping mound, I'll tell you the story about the dwarves and the net of doom."

Which will terrify the poor little hatchling! "Tell you what – I'll tell you both the story of the dwarves and the net of doom..." He crossed his eyes, and wobbled around on tip-talons, mimicking Wendell Bo's reedy whine, as he warbled, "Dooomy, do, do, do, doooom..."

Sammy Jo's shrill of laughter pealed through the chamber. "Granddad's funny!"

While Billy Bob rolled around on his sleep mound, messing up the bronze and silver coinage, hiccuping through his giggles.

He heard the sigh behind him. "Why didn't you ever laugh around me and Charlie Kay, Dad?"

"Because parenting's too important a thing to joke about. That's how it seemed to me and your mother."

"And grandparenting isn't?"

"You get a better sense of the things that need seriousness." *Like demanding due respect from annoyingly curious queenlings, for instance...* "And the things you can laugh about. Though they matter too." *Because laughing about the thing that terrifies said queenling will, hopefully, stop her chattering about it to her baby brother...*

He strolled towards the door. "For what it's worth, you and Rondell are doing just fine. Night, scatterlings. See you in the morning."

Emmy Lou's eyes widened. "Where are you going?"

"Thought me and Rondell could do with a heart to

heart." Castellan of old would have stretched out the pause. Soaked up the look of dread sweeping across her face. So it was a shock, when he found himself babbling, "I'm carrying more metal than is good for me. So... I wondered if he'd like to help lighten me up. Rake out some of the overlong scales and..."

"Ooo! Is Daddy going to eat up some of your yummy gold and silver?"

"Wan' yummy gold!" whined Billy Bob.

"That's not what Granddad is saying!" said Emmy Lou, sharply. "He's just teasing. Lords don't give away their precious metals just like that. They've fought hard for every glistening twinkle. And especially not to..." She bit her lip.

"The waste of skin and scales who ended up with your daughter," Rondell finished for her, from the main chamber, clambering clumsily to his feet. "While you finish disrespecting me in my own lair, I'm off to clear my head."

Smoke trickled from his nostrils as he straightened up. "And when all of you have finished putting your words into my mouth – maybe I can claw in a word or two of my own!" He glared at the lot of them as the family stared, wide-eyed, all crouching submissively. Even Emmy Lou.

"As I was *saying* – maybe Rondell wouldn't mind helping me shed some of my heavier scales, rather than trying to fly off in a huff." He glared at the waste of skin and scales. "Because if you're able to take off after the meal you've just had, I'll eat my own tail."

Sammy Jo snickered.

He decided to ignore her, continuing to skewer

Rondell to the floor with his gaze. "There's a fair amount of metal in amongst the scales I need to shed and – yes – as it happens, I was about to offer it, for you to consume."

Rondell blinked at him like a snake-tranced rabbit, evidently too shocked to respond.

"Does consume mean eat, Mummy?"

"Sammy Jo, will you be quiet!" hissed Emmy Lou.

"But does it?"

"Yes!"

The dragonet huffed a sigh, her sleeping mound chinking as she settled down. "Thought so. So he'll gobble up Granddad's metal, cos Daddy isn't a picky eater and that'll make him into a big tough lord and Overlord Wendell Bo will be nice to him, once he shines like Granddad."

Castellan stared at the queenling as she closed her eyes, twitched her wings and drifted off, evidently exhausted after her eventful day. Which hadn't stopped her announcing his Plan Four to the rest of the family, before he'd had a chance to explain it, himself.

He sighed. The pesky lizard was far too like her grandmother for comfort. Just as well he was going to stick around to keep her out of trouble.

The End

If you have enjoyed the story, please consider leaving a review, as it really helps writers like myself to spread the word about my books. Read on for a sneak peek at the first book in The Arcadian Chronicles series, *Mantivore Dreams*...

CHAPTER ONE

I held my breath. At last! I'd begun to think I'd never track down this music site. A picklist unfolded and I gawked at the strange words. Classical. Youth Cultures. Popular Cultures. Devotional. Ethnic.

What did they mean? Surely music was just a dance tune, or a song? I jabbed at the first one. Yet another picklist unpeeled onto the mat. Much longer. The words tasted strange as I sounded the musicians' names aloud. "Beethave- no -hoven... Mozz-art...Ta-ch— simply don't have the time to sound that one out." I went for a short name – Bach. *What did his Family do, to earn a Name like that?*

My eyes slid down the picklist of his tunes and found a piece about organs with something about a minor D. Probably a comedy. I hoped so – I could do with a laugh.

"Play." I breathed in the thick, sweet smell, storing up the sensation of Facs-mining on the Node – something I didn't do nearly enough. Looking across at the bubbling organi-packs glowing in their transparent tanks, I wished I could spend more time here, rather than snatch these forbidden stints when Mother was away.

The sound pealed out. What was the instrument? The notes seemed to stop, then to stack up on each other as they roared around the room, making Mother's flower vases buzz on the stone floor. It was unlike anything I'd ever heard. Torrents of melody attacked, drowning me in a rush of yearning. Everything seemed bright, and achingly beautiful.

The final crashing chord faded into silence.

Vrox sways, crooning with delight...

"Again." I closed my eyes as the monumental music thundered around me. I was Tranced by Vrox's joy as his emotion rolled through me, swept along by the reverberating climax—

I was stunned by a hard blow. And another. My hurt-hot ear rang with the impact. My cheek felt numb and heavy; my mouth filled with blood.

Vrox rears up, startled – sorry he hadn't noticed her approach...

"Turn it off! Turn it *off*!" Mother shrieked over the music. Her distorted face shivered in my vision for a shock-stalled eternity. Snatches of her rant filtered through Bach's bone-buzzing crescendo, making her fury seem even worse, "...-icked girl... -ways think you know best... -*dare* to override my passwor..." The organ tune stopped abruptly, just as she screamed, "...ate you! *I hate you...*"

Her words echoed horribly in the small room.

I jerked to my feet. *She's finally admitted it.* Axe-sharp hurt immediately snuffed out the flicker of relief, that I'd been right all these years. "Think I don't know?"

My voice shook, on the edge of tears. But grown girls of seventeen shouldn't cry in front of their mothers. I spun round, stumbling over a vase, and ran. Out into the hot sunlight. Past the stable, whose sharp smell reminded me I still hadn't mucked out the camel stall or goat pens. I scrabbled at the keycode on the sidegate, my shaking fingers making a hash of it.

She ran after me, yelling my name. Her panting echoed between the house and high fence, getting closer. Finally, as Vrox focused, I got the sequence right. The gate snicked open as she grabbed for my arm. I twisted away, the burn of her nails raking my skin. Skidding through the gate, I slammed it shut in her face. I sprinted across the front yard and past the first startled Node enquirer of the day, over the village courtyard, heading for Westgate. Heat settled like a greasy coat as I raced down Main Street, dust clotting my nose and throat.

At Westgate, Cupert Peaceman, the village security guard, dodged out of the way. Just as well, because I wasn't stopping for him, or anyone else. Ignoring several calls, driven by the need to get away, I finally slowed, winded and hurting, on the open road where the verges were widened to discourage hostile wildlife. The sun beat down in a suffocating sheet.

Haven't got a sunscreen – better find some shade. I tottered along on chewed-string legs, coughing up dust. *Mother would say it was my punishment.* The thought of her pushed me on.

Turning onto Mantivore Way was a relief. The palm tree clumps offered shade and the smell of the water strengthened my legs. I pushed through the shoulder-high reeds, which used to swish over my head, swallowing me whole. Moist leaves slapped against my sore legs. I broke off a brown-brittled stem, whipping it around and stamping noisily to frighten off any lone jaspers or nemmets sheltering from the sun. River silt seeped through my sandals, soothing my feet as I paddled in the murky water. Reaching my sanctuary – a stranded treetrunk – I sat down and rested my eyes on the river.

ACKNOWLEDGEMENTS

I would like to thank Camille Gooderham Campbell and the team over at *Every Day Fiction* for scooping 'Picky Eaters' out of the slush pile and publishing it as a 1,000 word short story way back in 2009. *Every Day Fiction* is a wonderful online magazine that publishes a new story every day and is still going strong.

I would like to acknowledge the enthusiasm of my grandchildren, Ethen and Oscar, who both enjoyed this one and were very keen to hear the longer version. If it hadn't been for Ethan's regular, 'Have you published *Picky Eaters*, yet, Gran?' there's a good chance this one would be languishing at the back of a virtual drawer with the time-travelling issues still a snarled mess.

I would like to thank the support and advice of my Writing Group – Sarah Palmer, Katie Glover, Debbie Watkins, Geoff Allnutt, and Liz Tait – for their encouragement and feedback. Managing to keep our group going via Zoom has been so important.

Massive thanks go to writing buddy and cover artist, Mhairi Simpson, for not only designing an awesome cover – but donating her time and effort free of charge, when she learnt I was donating the proceeds to mental health charities.

Huge dollops of gratitude go to my long-suffering husband, John, for reading through several versions of this one, helping me to unravel the timey-wimey problems and provide endless cups of tea, meals and industrial quantities of support

Thank you to my regular readers, whose interest in the exploits of Lizzy and Kyrillia make all the work worth it.

ABOUT THE AUTHOR

Born the same year as the Russians launched Sputnik, Sarah confidently expected that by the time she reached adulthood, the human race would have a pioneer colony on the Moon and be heading off towards Mars. So she was at a loss to know what to do once she realised the Final Frontier wasn't an option and rather lost her head - Sarah tried a lot of jobs she didn't like and married a totally unsuitable man.

Now she's finally come to terms with the fact that she'll never leave Earth, she has a lovely time writing science fiction and fantasy novels, having recently stepped down from teaching Creative Writing at Northbrook Metropolitan College in Worthing for the past ten years. Sarah lives in Littlehampton on the English south coast with a wonderful husband and a ridiculous number of books. She can be found online chatting about books at her book review blog https://sjhigbee.wordpress.com/ and you're very welcome to visit onto her website www.sjhigbee.com and her Facebook page https://www.facebook.com/sjhigbeeauthor/.